This book is given with love:

_____

_____

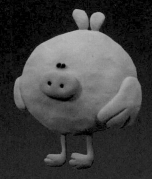

www.PigBird.co.uk

A Right Royal
Sprout

CREATED BY *Trevor Hardy* & *Neil James*

POEM BY *Frankie Wohler*

The palace is preparing for a right royal feast,

The queen has asked fifty people at least

To her Christmas Eve banquet in the glittering hall,

With turkey, plum pudding, and champagne for all.

December arrives with a sprinkling of snow,
The lights are all up and the castle's aglow.
Each room has a tree with baubles and bells,
And the kitchens are bursting with Christmassy smells.

Early in the morning of the right royal do,

Cook rushes 'round checking everything through.

"Now who did I ask to peel the sprouts?"

"Me!" gasps the maid. "They won't go without."

The sprouts are delighted to join in the fun,

They each reach the table except for just one.

Poor little Ralfie's not happy at all,

He's been thrown in the trash because he's too small.

But a sprout is a sprout and soon Ralfie jumps out,

Waiting in the shadows to see who's about.

There's only the maid and he gives her the slip,

No way was he going to end up on the tip.

Ralfie's out of the kitchen and off on the loose,
When who should he meet but a Canada Goose.
One of her babies is stuck in a pot,
She's very upset and honking a lot.

"Don't panic!" shouts Ralfie above all the din,
He's spotted a hole and soon squeezes in.
"I'm plucking your feathers!" and like it or not,
A much thinner baby pops out of the pot.

High on the hill where the snow lies so thick,

Ralfie bumps into a snowman waving a stick.

"Help me! Help me!" the poor fellow cries,

"I can't see a thing, someone's stolen my eyes."

Ralfie looks up and there in a tree,

He spies a young squirrel laughing with glee.

"Drop those at once. I know you're the thief."

And down plop the eyes to the snowman's relief.

With a hop and a skip Ralfie goes on his way,

And meets a red robin with plenty to say.

"Have you seen the old lady asleep by the gate?

She needs to wake up before it's too late."

"I tried lots of chirping an hour ago,"
The robin explains, bobbing 'round in the snow.
"I can see you're a really reliable sprout,
I'll leave it to you to work something out."

As 'Away In A Manger' rings out in the square,

Ralfie runs to the children and cries in despair,

"Louder! Sing louder!" and before very long

The lady wakes up and joins in their song.

As darkness descends Ralfie's all on his own,

When he suddenly hears an almighty groan.

"Help!" yells a man dangling down from a wall.

"It's Santa!" gasps Ralfie. "I can't let him fall!"

To add to his horror Ralfie sees clouds of smoke,

The building's on fire, Santa's starting to choke.

But what can he do? He's only a sprout,

Bruised at the edges and feeling worn out.

With no time to lose Ralfie thinks of a plan,

And sprints to the fire station as fast as he can.

He climbs on the desk and sounds the alarm.

"We're coming little sprout, you need to stay calm."

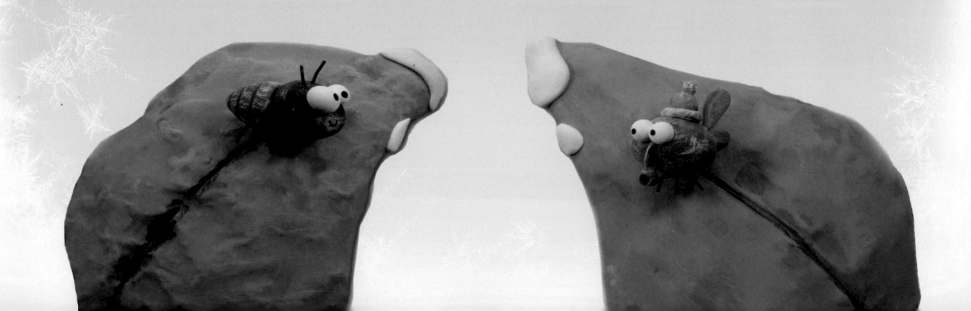

The blue lights are flashing, it's all systems go,

Ralfie sits with the driver as they plow through the snow.

Using ladders and ropes they save Santa first,

And beaming with pride, Ralfie's ready to burst.

Santa scoops Ralfie up and they're off on his sleigh,
To deliver the presents before Christmas Day.
"So tell me young sprout why you're out in the cold?"
With tears in his eyes, Ralfie's story is told.

"Ho! Ho! Ho! You're amazing, you deserve to be king,
And if I might mention just one other thing...
We'll party my friend so the whole world can see,
You'll always be a right royal sprout to me."

And me!

MEET THE AUTHORS

Trevor Hardy

Trevor is a multi-award winning stop-motion animator and writer. He lives in the UK with his wife and son. Trevor owns a stop-motion studio called 'Pigbird'.

Neil James

Neil is an actor, writer, and voice artist. He has written for TV, cinema, theatre, and is now thrilled to be working on books too. Neil has a huge passion for film, television, and music and also enjoys football, tennis, long walks, cold beer, and Christmas! He lives on the south coast of England with his family.

Frankie Wohler

Frankie was a school teacher for a number of years. Since her retirement, she has written a children's novel and had her first anthology of poems published in 2018. Frankie enjoys music, theatre, and walking in the English countryside with her husband, Ron.

HOW THE BOOK WAS MADE

Cameras set up to capture each scene

"My name is Trevor Hardy and thank you so much for purchasing my book, 'A Right Royal Sprout'.

I run a stop-motion animation studio called 'Pigbird' in the UK. Everything in 'A Right Royal Sprout' is hand-made. Each model, prop, and set is lovingly crafted from scratch using modeling clay. Once each set/scene is made, the characters are carefully positioned and the scene is lit to create the mood. The little props are added around them - like carrots, pots, and pans - and then, once ready and perfect, it is photographed.

This book was great fun to make and I really hope it catches the hearts of you readers, and delights every child that lovingly looks at the pictures, the characters, and the fantastic Christmas story."

– Trevor Hardy

Pigbird studios entrance

Scenes are carefully staged